To Ethen, Carmine, and Victoria

Adventure awaits...

Lil' LIBROS

www.LilLibros.com

My Pet Flamingo
Published by Little Libros, LLC

Text © 2023 Mariana Galvez
Art © 2023 Mariana Galvez
Colors and Design by Haydeé Yañez

Library of Congress Control Number 2022935546

Printed in China
Second Edition – 2023   JHP 10/23
27 26 25 24 23   2 3 4 5
ISBN 978-1-948066-53-2

Valentina's
Pet Flamingo
Guide

My Pet
Flamingo

by Mariana Galvez

If you find yourself with a pet flamingo,
there are many things you should know.
My pet flamingo Rosita taught me many lessons.
I've listed the most important ones below.

Si quieres un flamenco de mascota para tener,
hay muchas cosas que debes tú saber.
Rosita, mi flamenco, me enseñó una que otra cosa.
Las más importantes las enumero aquí, así que toma nota.

Pet flamingos enjoy cooking.
Breakfast is their favorite meal.
Make sure it's served in pink plates and cups.
Never the color teal.

Los flamencos disfrutan cocinar.
Su momento favorito es desayunar.
Asegúrate de que se sirva en tacitas y platitos rosados.
Y nunca en vajilla color verde azulado.

Pet flamingos love to swim outdoors
under bright tropical leaves.
On the shore, they snack on quesadillas and horchata.
They dislike any food with seeds.

A los flamencos mascota les encanta nadar
bajo hojas tropicales que el sol hace brillar.
En la orilla, toman horchata y pican quesadillas.
No les gusta ningún alimento con semillas.

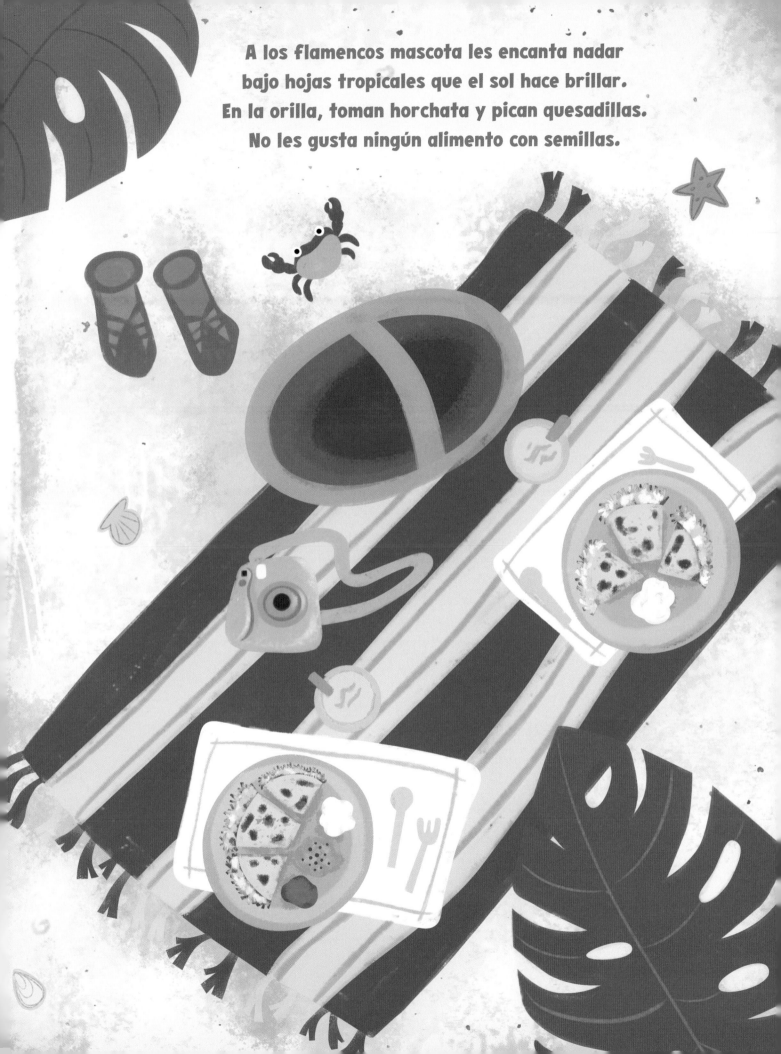

Pet flamingos shiver in the cold.
They dislike the hail or snow.
They enjoy nights by a cozy campfire,
making s'mores with extra pink marshmallows.

A los flamencos mascota el frío los hace temblar.
No les gusta el granizo ni cuándo va a nevar.
Disfrutan de las noches junto a una cálida fogata,
asan malvaviscos servidos con galletas y chocolate en barra.

Pet flamingos love to garden.
They'll use all the garden tools.
You'll need to remind them to clean up
even though they dislike this rule.

Les encanta la jardinería.
Usan bien las herramientas.
Pero yo que tú limpiar siempre les pediría,
aunque no les gusta cuando los escarmientas.

They'll take out all the measuring cups and spoons.
Pet flamingos love to bake.

Sacarán todas las tazas y cucharitas medidoras.
Pues hornear es lo que ellos más adoran.

Pet flamingos enjoy teatime and having friends over for cake.

Los flamencos disfrutan la hora del té
e invitar a amigos a comer pastel.

Pet flamingos love to dance ballet.
They love to sparkle and glow.
You'll need to sew them a new tutu outfit...

A los flamencos les encanta bailar ballet.
Brillar y resplandecer les fascina.
Tendrás que coserles un nuevo traje de tutú y corsé...

...for their ballerina debut recital!

Pet flamingos love planning picnics.
They'll fill a basket or two.
They won't forget the aguas frescas
or the chocolate fondue.

Los flamencos aman salir de excursión.
Y llenarán de comida un par de cestas.
No olvidarán las jarras de aguas frescas
o la fondue de chocolate para endulzar la ocasión.

Pet flamingos like trips to the library.
They'll take a mountain of books home.
You'll need to read them stories in the afternoon.
They don't like to read alone.

A los flamencos les agrada ir a la biblioteca.
Se llevarán una montaña de libros a tu casa.
Tendrás que leerles cuentos antes de la siesta.
Pues no les gusta si esto se te pasa.

Pet flamingos love bubble baths.
They'll take all their toys into the tub –
their boats, submarines, toy whale,
and their favorite octopus named Bubs.

Les encantan los baños de burbujas.
Llevarán todos sus juguetes a la bañera –
sus barcos, submarinos, ballenas y tortugas,
y su pulpo favorito Bubs no puede quedarse fuera.

Pet flamingos like to be tucked in at night
and want a kiss on their forehead.
You'll remind them to stay in their bed...

A los flamencos les gusta que los arropen por la noche
y quieren un beso en la frente antes de medianoche.
Les recordarás que se queden en su cama...

...but they'll run back to yours instead.

... pero volverán corriendo a tu cuarto en pijamas.

Pet flamingos make the very best friends.
Always and forever!
Adventure is near when they're around.
Life is better together.

Valentina's Pet Flamingo Guide

Los flamencos mascota son los mejores amigos.
¡Por siempre jamás!
Las aventuras no faltarán cuando estén contigo.
Juntos la vida mejor será.

rosita's pancake recipe

Author's Bio

Mariana Galvez was born in Mexico and grew up in South Los Angeles. In her childhood, it was during weekend trips to the library that her love for illustrating and writing was forged. After a number of years in the corporate world, she was called back to illustrating when creating art for her three children. She is the artist behind *Little Astrology Catrinas*. She currently resides in Whittier, CA with her husband where she loves to garden, cook vegan food, and chase after her beloved dog and cat.

Author's Note

Being a good friend is a valuable ability that children learn as they grow. In *My Pet Flamingo*, Valentina befriends a flamingo named Rosita and creates a guide on how to care for her flamingo based on a list of rules. These rules, although kooky and ultra specific, lean into the most important and unspoken rule of all: to treat flamingos with kindness and respect. By treating all the pets we come across with kindness and respect, we open our arms to a lasting friendship that will stand the test of time...and give us a companion for life.